# The Adventures Of posh princess

# AT THE ROYAL PALACE

written by Carolina Cutruzzola

illustrated by Mike Motz

www.poshprincessadventures.com

# Dedication

This book is dedicated to my wonderful husband Peter and my three little sweethearts Alissia, Marina and Luca. Thank you so much for your unconditional love, all the joy you bring to my life and for always believing in me! I love you.

# Acknowledgments

I have put a lot of love and special attention into this lovely book. I hope that you will enjoy reading it as much as I have enjoyed writing it! Cheers!

Eternal gratitude to our heavenly Father.
Through Him all things are possible.

Special thanks to my family and friends, in particular, the Consiglio's, the Cino's and the Cutruzzola's for their inspiration and support.

Thank you to Mike Motz and his magnificent team for capturing my vision for this book with your beautiful illustrations.

Thank you Ceilidh Marlow and the staff at FriesenPress who have helped make this process as smooth as possible and for helping to make my dream become a reality.

# Hello my princess friend!

My name is Posh Princess, and I live in a magical place called Princesstowne.

I like going to school and playing with my many princess friends. Though I enjoy being silly, I am also a very proper and polite little princess. I love glamour and fashion, but most of all I love, love, love adventures!

Today is a very special day! King Peter and Queen Caroline have invited my parents and me to the royal palace for tea. Oh, how I adore going to the palace! It sits on the highest mountain and can be seen from miles away. It is so magnificent and magical.

Princesstowne!

For a long time, the king and queen only had boys, but they always dreamed of having a little princess. One day, their dream came true: The royal princess, Madeline, was born. The king then changed the name of our town from King City to **Princesstowne**, and declared all the little girls in Princesstowne to be true princesses. Everybody in the land rejoiced and was happy!

As we arrived at the front door, King Peter greeted us with a strong handshake; the Queen gave each of us a nice, warm hug.

"Pardon me, Queen Caroline—where is Royal Princess Madeline?" I asked.

"She will be back shortly," she answered. "She is riding her horse out back."

The King and Queen led us to the parlour, where they offered us refreshments. I enjoyed some cold pink lemonade and yummy cookies while I waited for my friend to arrive.

At last, Royal Princess Madeline burst into the parlour.

"Where is Posh Princess?" she shouted.

We ran to each other and hugged. I was so glad to see one of my very best friends!

"Do you want to play?" asked Princess Madeline.

"Yes, please!" I answered.

We strolled off to the toy room together, hopping and skipping the entire way.

Royal Princess Madeline had many amazing toys and fun games. However, there was something very peculiar and mysterious in her toy room.

In the corner of the room, there was a large square; on the wall, above the square, was a pink crystal button. I had noticed it before, but had never said anything about it. I decided that today was the day that I would ask my friend about it, and so I did.

Royal Princess Madeline looked around to make sure that nobody was near.

"You'll never guess in **a million years**," she whispered.

"Please tell me—pretty, pretty please! I promise not to tell," I whispered back.

"Alright, today is your lucky day!" she said. "But I'm not going to tell you—I'm going to show you. Let's stand on the square together. I'll push the crystal button while you hold onto me."

"One, two, three," she counted out loud. Then she pressed the pink crystal button.

# Whooooosh! The floor dropped from beneath our feet.
Down we slid on the longest and most twisty slide that I had ever been on.

"Whee!" I shouted in excitement as we twirled around and around down the super-long slide.

When we finally reached the bottom, I asked, "Where are we?"

"Follow me!" she replied.

We walked through a short trail that led us to the biggest, most divine garden and swimming pool that I had ever seen. You will not believe what I saw in the swimming pool!

There were **three** mermaids, **two** dolphins, and a **pink** hippopotamus. I couldn't believe my eyes!

"Is this real? Am I dreaming?" I asked. "I'd better pinch myself OUCH! Yes, it sure is real, and it's marvellous!"

"I love to hang out here in my spare time," said Princess Madeline. "All of these sea creatures are my dearest friends. But no one outside the royal palace knows about them. You must keep this a secret!"

"I promise, dear friend," I said. "Your **secret** is **safe** with me!"

"I must admit, these magnificent creatures make me a little shy and nervous. Can they talk? Do you think they will want to be my friend? They are all so very different—how do they live together so peacefully?" I asked.

"Of course they can talk—they are very **magical!**" said Princess Madeline. "Don't worry or be nervous; they are very friendly. They love and accept each other, even though they are so different. That is what makes them so beautiful."

All of the sudden, the three mermaids popped up in front of us.

"Hi, I'm Melanie," said one, "and these are my sisters, Marta and Melissa."

"Nice to meet you," I answered. "I'm Posh Princess."

Oh my, oh my, I could not believe that I was talking to the mermaids. They were so beautiful!

"Would you like to come for a swim with us?" Melanie asked.

"I'd love to, but I didn't bring a swimsuit" I responded sadly.

"Your wish is my command!" exclaimed Princess Madeline as she dangled two pretty bathing suits.

**"Yippee!"** we all shouted.

We quickly changed into our swimsuits and jumped into the pool.
We had such a ball swimming and playing with the mermaids.

Just then, a dolphin popped up from beneath me and took me for a ride on her back!

"Hello! My name is Delilah," she said, "and that is my sister Dorothy."

How exciting! I had never ridden on a dolphin before. What a dream come true!

Next, the cute hippopotamus swam over to me.

"Hello, my name is Princess Harriet the Hippo!" she said.

"It's very nice to meet you!" I answered.

She wiggled her ears at me; it was so funny and sweet!

All too soon, the sun began to set, and it was time to go. I was sad to say goodbye to all my new fabulous friends. They were so friendly and welcoming. As it turned out, I had nothing to be shy about after all!

I thanked Royal Princess Madeline for such a special day as we walked through a trail that lead us back to the palace.

This was the most fun and exciting adventure I had ever had at the royal palace. I hope that you enjoyed it, too! I can't wait for you to join me on my next exciting adventure!

The End

Produced by:


FriesenPress

Suite 300 – 852 Fort Street
Victoria, BC, Canada V8W 1H8

www.friesenpress.com

Distributed to the trade by The Ingram Book Company